Scholastic Book Clubs

Chapters

A Special Sampling
of Novels by
Newbery Authors

SCHOLASTIC
BOOK CLUBS
CHAPTERS

At Scholastic Book Clubs, it is our mission to help teachers introduce students to the joys of quality literature. We suggest you try reading these selections aloud to your class. We believe that giving students a preview of excellent stories is sometimes the best way to spark their interest in reading—and that's why we created this special volume.

Written by six acclaimed Newbery-winning authors, the books excerpted here are filled with unforgettable characters and powerful stories. Told in a way that encourages both emotional and intellectual involvement, these selections have strong appeal for today's students. They include a variety of genres and subject matter to captivate young readers and leave them eagerly waiting for more.

THE ART OF KEEPING COOL

Ages 10 and Up

IT'S 1942, AND ROBERT'S FATHER is away fighting the war, so Robert and his family move to Rhode Island to stay with grandparents he's never met. There, the thirteen-year-old uncovers a world of secrets and mysteries—both inside and outside the family. Why doesn't his hot-tempered grandfather ever mention Robert's father? And why does his cousin Elliot hide his artistic talents from the family? Are there really German submarines hiding right off the coast? Could the strange neighbor with a German accent be a Nazi spy?

JANET TAYLOR LISLE's many books for young readers include *Afternoon of the Elves*, a Newbery Honor Book, *The Lampfish of Twill*, *The Lost Flower Children*, and *Forest*, as well as *A Message from the Match Girl*, part of her Investigators of the Unknown series.

THE ART OF KEEPING COOL

Excerpt: Chapter 1

Janet Taylor Lisle

**E**ARLY SATURDAY MORNING WE heard the big guns were pulling close to Sachem's Head.

The word was they'd begin passing through town sometime between ten and eleven o'clock, so my cousin Elliot and I walked up Parson's Lane right after breakfast. We stood along the side of West Main Road with a raw sea wind whipping past our ears and it wasn't long before we got so cold we had to start hopping.

"Hey Robert, did we have to get here so early?" Elliot panted between hops.

"We had to," I panted back. "It's going to be history."

This was early March 1942, barely three months after Pearl Harbor was bombed and America went to war against the Nazis and the Japanese, and we weren't the only ones on the road that morning. Soon people began to stream out from everywhere and wait at the ends of their driveways. Kids were climbing trees to look up the road. Every so often somebody would ride by in a car or on a bike and yell out a progress report. They're at Wickham Road, won't be long now! They're up to Mrs. Grinnell's!

There was no need to worry. Each gun was chained on two—not one but two—flatbed haulers because it was so huge, and the trucks that pulled the flatbeds were overwhelmed by their loads and inched forward with agonized groans and shudders, even going downhill.

A two-year-old child could have walked faster, someone said.

And done less damage to the road, someone else observed.

Across the way, I saw a tall, boney man in a blue cap take a notepad out of his knapsack and bend to write in it. I thought he was a reporter from one of the Providence newspapers, and felt proud to be there at such a momentous event.

The guns had been statewide news all week. They had already been two days on the road coming from the Riverton train depot, ten miles away, and would require another half day to haul to Fort Brooks. Along their route, a bridge had been reconstructed over an inlet to accommodate their weight. A yapping dog had darted too close and been crushed under one of the flatbed's slow-moving wheels. Marion Wainright, a local pacifist, had threatened to throw herself under another wheel. She was arrested and taken away to the police station to cool her heels. People weren't so tolerant of freethinkers back then, especially in a New England coastal village where the world hadn't yet shown much of a face.

They were mighty sixteen-inch bore naval guns, two of them—the largest and most powerful long-range weapons at that time. I'll never forget how the first tremendous body rose over the hill, its long, gray barrel pointed back up the road. An escort of armed soldiers walked soberly alongside.

"Stand back," I told Elliot. "It might speed up coming down."

These were not the first guns to be brought down the

road. The fort complex—there were actually three bat-teries, each looking out to sea in a different direction—had been quietly accumulating artillery and soldiers for several months. But they were by far the largest weapons, the farthest shooting, and not a sight to miss if you were interested in the tools of war, as I was.

Most folks out that morning had heard a pretty close description of what they were going to see, and they still caught their breaths when the guns came over the hill. They edged away from the road as each gun's 143 tons and sixty-eight feet of molded steel rattled and clanked and cracked the macadam going by on the way to the job of protecting us, and the Rhode Island coast, from the Germans.

The war hadn't scared me yet and it didn't scare me that morning, I was glad to find out. My father was fly-ing with the Royal Canadian Air Force out of England. He was one of the first Americans to go overseas. The country was gearing up, preparing to fight. I was impressed all right—"Elliot, look at those monsters!"—but I stood my ground as the guns rolled toward us down the hill, even when the earth began to rumble and shake under our feet. Turning, I saw my cousin Elliot's face empty of every emotion except terror.

"El, it's okay. They're not going to shoot."

Elliot had a problem—he registered things too deep. Sometimes it seemed to me as if his receivers were turned up too high on the world, and what he saw and heard came at him with extra force. These days, he mostly knows how to hide it. He's made it out and been around, picked up a name for himself, though like any-body, he can get caught off guard sometimes. He'll look too far or see too small and find himself on the verge of panic. But he's mastered the art of keeping cool and can put up a good defense so no one can tell.

Back in the spring of 1942, when we were both thir-teen years old, Elliot Marks didn't have many defenses, and I could look in his eyes and see everything he was feeling.

"Really, you don't have to be scared."

"Who's scared?" Elliot lied, chewing deep into his hand. When he got nervous, he had a tic of biting into the L-shaped place between his thumb and his first fin-ger. Not a hard bite, just a sort of rhythmic gnawing. He was no coward, though. That day he stayed with me, following the flatbeds down to where they turned in at the gate to the fort.

A private was on duty at the guardhouse and wouldn't let us through. We hung around looking for empty Coke bottles in the tall grass where the soldiers tossed them going by in their Jeeps. Six empties could get you five cents at the store in town. We didn't find any and, with nothing else doing at the fort, we set off for home, taking a back route along the beaches.

"I'm going to draw those guns as soon as I get home," Elliot said. Even then he could draw anything, just from looking at it once.

"I'm going to ask your dad if he can get us in to see them," I told him. "Their shells weigh a ton. A ton! Can you believe it?"

Elliot's father was a plumber and he had a government contract to work at the fort. It was the thing that was saving Elliot's parents, moneywise, that year.

"He can't get you in," Elliot said. "You can only get in for special stuff, like the movies."

"Well, somehow I'm getting in. Those guns can shoot

twenty-six miles—that's over Martha's Vineyard."

"Mike Parini told me he saw a German sub," Elliot suddenly remembered.

"Where?"

"Off South Shore, toward the islands. Not the whole thing—the periscope coming up. But it was probably a lobster buoy or something."

"It might have been a sub," I said. "They're out there. They torpedoed that tanker off Newport in January. You know they're looking for more hits. They'd invade us if they could. These guns are getting here just in time."

"These guns," Elliot said, shaking his head, "these guns are..." He stopped walking, and I saw his face go into the same freeze as when he'd first seen the long gray barrels come over the hill.

"Come on, El, don't do that."

Elliot started walking again, but he wouldn't talk. Except once he came to a halt and asked, "Hey Robert, did you see that guy?"

"What guy?"

"When the guns were coming, the big, skinny guy across the road in the blue cap? That was Abel Hoffman, the painter. He was famous over there."

"Over where? Abel who?" I asked, three times in a row. But Elliot had gone into another of his shut-downs and wouldn't answer. Low under his breath, I heard him mutter:

"I'm drawing them, that's what I'm doing. As soon as we're home, I'm getting them down."

THE TIME BIKE
Ages 9 and Up

FOR HIS BIRTHDAY, Eddy Hall receives the expensive bike of his dreams—only to have it stolen the very next day! Then a huge package arrives from Eddy's royal uncle in India. Inside is an old-fashioned bicycle with a wicker basket—the kind of bike no self-respecting boy like Eddy would be caught dead riding. But he's about to discover that his bike has some very strange and amazing powers...and before long he'll be traveling through time on the ride of his life!

JANE LANGTON has written six adventures starring the Hall family, including the Newbery Honor-winning *The Fledgling*, as well as *The Diamond in the Window* and *The Fragile Flag*.

THE
TIME BIKE

Excerpt: Chapter 6

Jane Langton

**T**HREE DAYS WENT BY, AND THE bicycle from India was still in the front hall beside the stairs, in the way.

"Eddy," said Uncle Freddy, "would you move it? Why not put it on the front porch where you kept the other one? But lock it to the railing this time."

So it won't be stolen? Eddy smiled grimly. Who would steal such a dumb old bike? But even so, he didn't put it on the front porch where anybody could see it. He found a perfect hiding place for it, a shadowy triangular nook next to the coat closet under the front hall stairs.

It was just the right size, and it had a crimson velvet curtain on a drawstring that hid his skateboard and Uncle Freddy's old golf bag and a croquet set with a couple of broken mallets.

Laboriously, Eddy carried the old stuff up to the attic. Then he wheeled his shameful new bicycle into the space behind the curtain.

In the dark it gleamed a little, the way his old rocket model had glowed in the dark because phosphorescent stuff was mixed with the plastic. His embarrassing new bicycle must be coated with phosphorescent paint.

It trembled slightly under his hands as he propped it upright, almost as if it were alive. Little sparkles flickered around the rims of the wheels. And there was a sound, a kind of whispering murmur.

Eddy pulled the curtain aside to let in light and peered at the dial mounted on the handlebars. It wasn't a speedometer—it was a clock. And there was a dome-shaped bell on top, just like the one on an old-fashioned alarm clock. The whole thing looked just like a clock in a cartoon, the kind that bounces up and down when the alarm goes off.

He looked more closely at the dial. How weird! It didn't say 1, 2, 3, 4, all the way to 12. In fact, there were two dials. The words printed on them were very small. One said:

Days

and the other:

Years

There were a great many little marks around the circle of the Days dial—probably 365 of them, decided

Eddy, one for every day of the year.

The Years dial was different. It went from 0 to 10 to 100 to 1,000 to 10,000 to 100,000. A hundred thousand years! What did it mean, a clock that told time in thousands of years?

And there was a tab at the side, some sort of on-off switch. No, it wasn't an on-off switch, it was a plus-and-minus switch. What did that mean, plus and minus?

"Why, Eddy," said Aunt Alex, suddenly appearing in the front hall with Eleanor, "what a lovely headlight. It sparkles like a diamond."

"It does?" Eddy looked. The rocket-shaped headlight on the front fender was just one more thing that was out of style. He tried to turn it off, but there was no switch.

"It reminds me of something," said Eleanor, narrowing her eyes, staring at it through her big glasses.

Eddy knew what she was thinking of—the big jewel that had once been part of the stained-glass window in the attic, that huge chunk of glass that had turned out in the end to be a diamond, a real diamond, so valuable that it was beyond price. "It's not much good without a switch," he said. "The battery will run down any minute."

"The one in back is pretty too," said Aunt Alex,

bending low over the rear fender, where the red reflector shone in the light of the desk lamp. "It's like a ruby, a real ruby." She stood up and smiled at Eddy. "It's like a bicycle from fairyland."

Then she went into the kitchen with Eleanor, and Eddy went back to studying his new bicycle with more interest than before.

He climbed on the seat to see what it felt like and dropped the curtain again. Now he was alone in the dark with the bike. In front of him the headlight shone on the wall of the coat closet, making a bright pattern like a star.

To his surprise it felt good to perch erect, high above the floor. It was sort of majestic and dignified, like riding an elephant.

Something white twirled in front of him—the tag on the handlebars. Eddy reached for it, but it kept fluttering and twisting. Finally he got it between his fingers. Pulling open the curtain, he looked at the tag. One side still said Srinagar, Kashmir. The other said:

TIME BIKE

Time Bike! What did it mean?

He could hear Aunt Alex talking quietly from the kitchen with Eleanor, who was complaining loudly about Amanda Upshaw's party.

"I still don't have an invitation! Becky's got one. Lisa's got one. It's only me, I'm the only one that hasn't got one. I mean, they've all got invitations already, all the best kids!"

There was a pause, and then Aunt Alex said, "What do you mean by 'best kids'?"

"Oh, you know, Aunt Alex. They're—oh, I don't know. If you could see them, you'd know what I mean."

"I see," said Aunt Alex.

Eddy stopped listening. What if he set the dial of the clock for some time in the past, like six months ago? Maybe it really was a time bike. Maybe it would really take him back to last December. Dreamily, he put his fingers on the setscrew that moved the hand of the dial that counted days.

Then he came to his senses. The idea was too scary. He should think it over first and then try it very carefully. Those people in fairy stories who were given three wishes always got in trouble. They wasted all three because they didn't think. He would be more careful.

But at that instant the little rooster in the backyard

crowed noisily, and the silly cuckoo popped out of the clock and squawked.

Eddy's hand jerked. The bicycle jiggled, and the bell went ding. There was a flash of lightning in the little round mirror on the handlebars, and a humming noise from the wheels as if they were going around.

It was only for a moment. Then the vibrations stopped. The dinging stopped. Eddy got off the bike and opened the curtain.

Through the oval window in the front door he could see the trees across the road, and the grass in the front yard. Everything was green. It was still June, not last December.

The bike was a failure. It didn't work. It wasn't a time bike. The strange dials didn't mean anything at all.

Aunt Alex and Eleanor were still talking in the kitchen.

"What do you mean by 'best kids'?" said Aunt Alex.

"Oh, you know, Aunt Alex. They're—oh, I don't know. If you could see them, you'd know what I mean."

"I see," said Aunt Alex.

THE CHRISTMAS RAT

Ages 9 and Up

IT'S CHRISTMAS VACATION. For most kids, that means fun-filled days of sleeping in and hanging out with friends and family. But not for Eric. His parents work all day, his best friend is in Florida, and he's already peeked at his presents—and they're not that great. Now he has to wait around his apartment for an exterminator to arrive. What Eric doesn't know is that the strange exterminator will soon sweep him into a fierce war against the rats—and that Eric himself will become the hunted!

AVI has written a wide range of books for children, from fantasies and historical adventures to tales of terror and sports stories. Some of his books include *The True Confessions of Charlotte Doyle* and *Nothing but the Truth*, both Newbery Honor winners, as well as *Poppy, Midnight Magic,* and *Perloo the Bold.*

THE
CHRISTMAS
RAT

Excerpt: Chapter 3, Section 2

Avi

**W**HO'S THERE?" I ASKED. IF YOU live in a city apartment you're always supposed to ask that before you open the door. Even grown-ups do it. You'd be amazed at the creeps that come into nice buildings like ours.

"Exterminator!" came the answer.

I flipped the dead bolt, plus the second lock, then pulled open the heavy door.

A huge guy was standing before me. I mean, he was really big. Underneath a black peaked cap that had a skull-with-wings logo, he had this straight, white-blond hair that reached to his shoulders. His face was long, pale, with a thin nose and glittering eyes. He had this wild mustache—whitish-blond—that stuck out on both sides of his face. The mustache reminded me of the long-horned cows I'd seen on a school video about the old West.

He was wearing a black leather jacket, fleece-lined. Black combat boots. Army issue, I figured. Each hand gripped the handle of a metal box. The boxes had the same picture of a skull-with-wings as his hat.

There was a smell about him, too. I couldn't place it.

"Folks home?" he asked in a voice that was low, sort of rumbly.

"They're working," I answered, staring up a him. "But they told me you were coming so I can let you in."

"Good," he said.

I stepped aside.

"Where's your kitchen?" he demanded.

"Over here," I said, and led the way.

When we got there the exterminator peered around with those sharp eyes of his. "What you got, dude? Roaches? Mice? Rats?"

"I think we're pretty clean," I said, wondering if he'd be disappointed.

"Nothing to do with cleanliness, kid," he snapped. "If the Queen of England lived around here, trust me, she'd have roaches." He pulled open his metal boxes, laying out canisters marked:

POISON! HARMFUL IF SWALLOWED! CAUTION! CAUSTIC!

"This is the city," he went on, all riled up. "Vermin live here. Fact is, there are more vermin than people.

Did you know that, kid?"

"Nope."

"Right. If it weren't for guys like me, the vermin would take over. Have any idea what would happen then?"

I shook my head.

"They would exterminate people."

"They would?"

"End of life as you know it. Hey, how come you're not in school?" he suddenly asked, fixing me with a hard stare.

"It's Christmas vacation."

"Wish I had a vacation. For me, it's war all the time. Otherwise the vermin would take over."

While he talked, he'd been busy sprinkling white powder along the base of the kitchen cabinets and inside closets and drawers. His bony, pale fingers opened everything. It was as if he had the right to go into all our hidden places.

I watched him for a while. Then I said, "Do you like your work?"

"Love it."

"How come?"

"People always ask me that," the exterminator said

without stopping his work with a box labeled *TOXIC!* "See, kid, I was in the military. Special Services. Trained to kill. Guns. Hand-to-hand. Locks. Not a lock in the world I can't open. Booby traps. Mines. Hand bombs. Chemicals. Even bugle blowing—you know, Taps. The works. You name it. That's all I knew. I was good at it, too.

"Anyway, I put in my time and then some. I'm not even allowed to tell you what I did. Trust me. I was everywhere.

"But, hey, nothing good lasts forever. Right? It was back to this world for me.

"Didn't take me long to figure out that unless I found a job which would let me kill—legal-like—I'd be in trouble. So I got me a job as an exterminator. It solved everything."

Though all his talk of killing made me feel uncomfortable, I had to admit, he was interesting.

"Hey, I like killing things," he went on as if reading my mind. "And you know what?" He poked a long finger in my direction. "The world likes what I'm doing. And another thing. I get money and respect for what I do."

All I could say was, "Oh."

He had finished the kitchen. "Show me the other rooms," he commanded.

I led the way.

"The hardest thing of all is rats," the exterminator continued. "The worst. I can tell you more about rats than you want to know. Filthy creatures. They spread diseases worse than any poison. You wouldn't believe what they steal. Not just small stuff, either."

I must have looked doubtful, because he said, "Hey, in the army, I once saw a rat roll a hand grenade away. They grab things that glitter. Or glow.

"Yeah, people don't know it, but rats have really influenced the world. Sure, sometimes for good, you know, in medical labs. But mostly for the worst. Trust me. Public Enemy Number One. Got any around here?"

"I don't think so."

"People think if you live in a nice neighborhood, no rats. Forget it. I used to work in Beverly Hills. You know, fancy Los Angeles? Huge shopping mall out there for rich folks? Well, it was mostly a resort for rats. Don't worry. I got 'em. Hey, if anyone brings on the end of the world it's going to be me, not them."

He opened one of his boxes and pulled out what I thought was a pistol. Fixed across the barrel at right angles was a miniature bow. It startled me.

"A crossbow," he explained. "I don't believe in using firearms outside the army. Anyway, knowing me," he added with a glare, as if I had just accused him of something, "I'm not so sure I could get a license. But, see, I can fit a bolt in here," he pointed to a slot grooved into the top of the gun barrel, "and shoot. It's pretty silent. Perfect for rats."

I stared at the weapon.

He quickly put the crossbow away, then whipped a business card out of his pocket and handed it to me. The card was red. The letters were printed in black.

Anjela Gabrail
Exterminator
225-5463
24-Hr Cell Phone

"You ever see a rat, kid, ring me. Anytime. Anywhere. Keep my cell phone by my pillow. I'll be there. People call me Anje. You know An-je. And trust me, I hate rats."

"Yes, sir," I said, putting his card in my pocket.

Anje was in the living room now, kneeling on the

floor, fiddling with a canister in the middle of the rug.

"Okay, kid," he went on. "Gas warfare time. I'm setting off this bomb. It'll fog the place with poison, killing the really small vermin. Lethal. Breathe it and it'll make you sick. So get out of here for twenty-five minutes. Or more. Go to a buddy's. Read a comic book in the hall. Anywhere but here. I'll shut the door behind us. Don't come back until time's up. But if you go outside, wrap yourself up tight. It's wicked."

Grabbing my coat, I watched as he twisted the cap off the fog bomb.

There was a hiss. A stream of fog shot into the air. It had a sour smell which I realized was what I had smelled when Anje first walked in.

"Take cover!" he shouted, and began to back away from the spewing bomb.

I ran for the door. The exterminator, steel cases in hand, followed me into the hallway. He slammed the door behind us. Then he unrolled a long strip of masking tape from his pocket and covered the cracks around the door. "Got a watch?" he asked.

"Yes."

"Remember," he said. "Nothing less than twenty-five minutes."

"Twenty-five minutes," I repeated.

"And if you see a rat, call me. You've got my number. You and me, we'll kill him, okay? Merry Christmas!"

"Merry Christmas," I replied.

STARGIRL

Ages 10 and Up

THERE'S AN UNSPOKEN RULE at Mica Area High School—don't stand out. That's why people can't stop talking about the new girl. Sophomore Stargirl Caraway dresses strangely, carries her pet rat around, and serenades other students with her ukulele in the middle of the school cafeteria. How long can a person like Stargirl last in this sea of conformity? One thing is for sure: After knowing Stargirl, Leo—and the school—will never be the same!

JERRY SPINELLI is the author of many best-selling books for young readers, including *Maniac Magee*, winner of the Newbery Medal; *Wringer*, winner of a Newbery Honor; *Crash* ; and *Knots in My Yo-yo String*, his autobiography.

STARGIRL

Excerpt: Chapter 2

Jerry Spinelli

**W**HEN WE GOT TO SCHOOL THE next day, Hillari Kimble was holding court at the door.

"She's not real," Hillari said. She was sneering. "She's an actress. It's a scam."

Someone called out, "Who's scamming us?"

"The administration. The principal. Who else? Who cares?" Hillari wagged her head at the absurdity of the question.

A hand flashed in the air: "Why?"

"School spirit," she spat back. "They think this place was too dead last year. They think if they plant some nutcase in with the students —"

"Like they plant narcs in schools!" someone else shouted.

Hillari glared at the speaker, then continued,

"—some nutcase who stirs things up, then maybe all the little students will go to a game once in a while or join a club."

"Instead of making out in the library!" chimed another voice. And everybody laughed and the bell rang and we went in.

Hillari Kimble's theory spread throughout the school and was widely accepted.

"You think Hillari's right?" Kevin asked me. "Stargirl's a plant?"

I snickered. "Listen to yourself."

He spread his arms. "What?"

"This is Mica Area High School," I reminded him. "It's not a CIA operation."

"Maybe not," he said, "but I hope Hillari's right."

"Why would you hope that? If she's not a real student, we can't have her on Hot Seat."

Kevin wagged his head and grinned. "As usual, Mr. Director, you fail to see the whole picture. We could use the show to expose her. Can't you see it?" He did the marquee thing with his hands: "Hot Seat Uncovers Faculty Hoax!"

I stared at him. "You want her to be a fake, don't you?"

He grinned ear to ear. "Absolutely. Our ratings will go sky-high!"

I had to admit, the more I saw of her, the easier it was to believe she was a plant, a joke, anything but real. On that second day she wore bright-red baggy shorts with a bib and shoulder straps—overall shorts. Her sandy hair was pulled back into twin plaited pigtails, each tied with a bright-red ribbon. A rouge smudge appled each cheek, and she had even dabbed some oversized freckles on her face. She looked like Heidi. Or Bo Peep.

At lunch she was alone again at her table. As before, when she finished eating, she took up her ukulele. But this time she didn't play. She got up and started walking among the tables. She stared at us. She stared at one face, then another and another. The kind of bold, I'm-looking-at-you stare you almost never get from people, especially strangers. She appeared to be looking for someone, and the whole lunchroom had become very uncomfortable.

As she approached our table, I thought: What if she's looking for me? The thought terrified me. So I turned from her. I looked at Kevin. I watched him grin goofily up at her. He wiggled his fingers at her and whispered, "Hi, Stargirl." I didn't hear an answer. I was intensely aware of her passing behind my chair.

She stopped two tables away. She was smiling at a pudding-bodied senior named Alan Ferko. The lunchroom was dead silent. She started strumming the uke. And singing. It was "Happy Birthday." When she came to his name she didn't sing just his first name, but his full name:

"Happy Birthday, dear Alan Fer-kooooh"

Alan Ferko's face turned red as Bo Peep's pigtail ribbons. There was a flurry of whistles and hoots, more for Alan Ferko's sake, I think, than hers. As Stargirl marched out, I could see Hillari Kimble across the lunchroom rising from her seat, pointing, saying something I could not hear.

"I'll tell you one thing," Kevin said as we joined the

mob in the hallways, "she better be fake."

I asked him what he meant.

"I mean if she's real, she's in big trouble. How long do you think somebody who's really like that is going to last around here?"

Good question.

Mica Area High School—MAHS—was not exactly a hotbed of nonconformity. There were individual variants here and there, of course, but within pretty narrow limits we all wore the same clothes, talked the same way, ate the same food, listened to the same music. Even our dorks and nerds had a MAHS stamp on them. If we happened to somehow distinguish ourselves, we quickly snapped back into place, like rubber bands.

Kevin was right. It was unthinkable that Stargirl could survive—or at least survive unchanged—among us. But it was also clear that Hillari Kimble was at least half right: this person calling herself Stargirl may or may not have been a faculty plant for school spirit, but whatever she was, she was not real.

She couldn't be.

Several times in those early weeks of September, she

showed up in something outrageous. A 1920s flapper dress. An Indian buckskin. A kimono. One day she wore a denim miniskirt with green stockings, and crawling up one leg was a parade of enamel ladybug and butterfly pins. "Normal" for her were long, floor-brushing pioneer dresses and skirts.

Every few days in the lunchroom she serenaded someone new with "Happy Birthday." I was glad my birthday was in the summer.

In the hallways, she said hello to perfect strangers. The seniors couldn't believe it. They had never seen a tenth-grader so bold.

In class she was always flapping her hand in the air, asking questions, though the question often had nothing to do with the subject. One day she asked a question about trolls—in U.S. History class.

She made up a song about isosceles triangles. She sang it to her Plane Geometry class. It was called "Three Sides Have I, But Only Two Are Equal."

She joined the cross-country team. Our home meets were held on the Mica Country Club golf course. Red flags showed the runners the way to go. In her first meet, out in the middle of the course, she turned left when everyone else turned right. They waited for her at the finish line. She never showed up. She was dismissed from the team.

One day a girl screamed in the hallway. She had seen a tiny brown face pop up from Stargirl's sunflower canvas bag. It was her pet rat. It rode to school in the bag every day.

One morning we had a rare rainfall. It came during her gym class. The teacher told everyone to come in. On the way to the next class they looked out the windows. Stargirl was still outside. In the rain. Dancing.

We wanted to define her, to wrap her up as we did each other, but we could not seem to get past "weird" and "strange" and "goofy." Her ways knocked us off balance. A single word seemed to hover in the cloudless sky over the school:

HUH?

Everything she did seemed to echo Hillari Kimble: She's not real… She's not real…

And each night in bed I thought of her as the moon came through my window. I could have lowered my shade to make it darker and easier to sleep, but I never did. In that moonlit hour, I acquired a sense of the otherness of things. I liked the feeling the moonlight gave me, as if it wasn't the opposite of day, but its underside, its private side, when the fabulous purred on my snow-white sheet like some dark cat come in from the desert.

It was during one of these nightmoon times that it came to me that Hillari Kimble was wrong. Stargirl was real.

STOWAWAY

Ages 9 and Up

IT'S 1768 AND ELEVEN-YEAR-OLD Nicholas Young has just hidden himself aboard a ship and is waiting to be carried far away from his miserable life in London. Little does the young stowaway know, but he is about to go on the most astonishing adventure of his life. The H.M.S. *Endeavour* and its captain, James Cook, are on a secret and dangerous mission to discover an unknown continent at the bottom of the globe! This fictional journal is based on a real-life stowaway on the *Endeavour*.

KAREN HESSE is the author of several books for children, including *Out of the Dust*, winner of the Newbery Medal and the Scott O'Dell Award, and the acclaimed books *Witness*, *The Music of Dolphins*, *Letters from Rifka*, and *Just Juice*.

STOWAWAY

Excerpt: Part 1

Karen Hesse

August 1768

SUNDAY 7th TO FRIDAY 19th *[Plymouth]* With the help of Seamen Francis Haite, John Ramsay, and Samuel Evans, I have managed to keep my presence aboard *Endeavour* secret. She's a small Bark, and her Company over eighty in number. It's a wonder I've not been discovered, with all the coming and going of the men aboard, but I have not. The three seamen I paid to get me on bring biscuit and water. They make certain I exercise each night during middle watch, when there are fewer hands on deck. But there is little to relieve my situation till *Endeavour* sails.

It's a good hiding place I've got, in the aft of what Samuel Evans calls the Pinnace, a small boat *Endeavour* carries aboard her. I can look over the edge and see the deck without being noticed. But it is difficult, lying still, day and night. Sometimes the urge to cry out nearly gets the better of me. I haven't yet. It would go hard on the men who have helped me if I did. And I would be returned to the Butcher, who would take it out of my hide, if Father didn't kill me first.

Endeavour creaks without rest as she sits at anchor.

The breeze chatters her ropes against the masts. The ship's bell clangs on the hour and half hour, and the bosun's whistle ever pierces the air with its piped orders. With all the din of London, I thought it could never be so noisy on a ship. But it is.

I've chickens for neighbours, and pigs, and a goat. They snort and cluck and bleat day and night, in pens on deck. I'm glad of their company and wish I might go near them more often. I've had milk out of the goat, straight from her teat. John Ramsay says she's aboard for the Gentlemen and Officers, so they might have fresh cream when they please.

Today, the 19th, Captain Cook gathered the Ship's Company on deck and read the Articles of War aloud. Captain is a clean-shaven man, strict and stern, with cold eyes. The Articles he read stated there would be no swearing of oaths on board, no drunkenness, nor uncleanness. Good thing Captain hasn't had a whiff of me. The Articles declare cowardice, mutiny, and deser- tion to be punishable acts. They say naught of stow- aways, but Francis Haite, John Ramsay, and Samuel Evans each glanced my way during Captain's reading.

SATURDAY 20th *[Plymouth]* Rain, rain, rain. Even with the cover pulled over me, I am thoroughly wet.

SUNDAY 21st *[Plymouth]* We toss at anchor. My stomach heaves and cramps and heaves again. And I'm bruised from head to toe.

I half wish Father would come aboard and take me home. I'm tired of being wet and hungry. Father knows by my letter that I've run out on the Butcher. But I did not write where I meant to go, nor what I meant to do, for when I sent the letter, I hardly knew my plans myself. Even if he knew, he would not come. I am a disappointment to Father. All my brothers are scholars. Only I could not settle to my studies. Father has no use for a son who will not learn his Latin.

MONDAY 22nd *[Plymouth]* A storm has made the sea sorely troubled beneath us, even as we sit at anchor. This noon a servant boy saw me heaving out of the Pinnace as he ran to be sick himself over the side. I pray he was too much in his own misery to take notice of me and mine.

TUESDAY 23rd *[Plymouth]* Last night the servant boy came right to my hiding place.

"Lad," he whispered, "are you still alive in there?"

I held silent. After a moment he poked his head into the Pinnace and stared straight at me. I stared straight back. He looked to be fifteen or sixteen years of age.

When he made out I was well, he smiled. Blisters, I have never seen such a beaming smile.

Samuel Evans called out from the forward of the ship. "Hey, there. You, boy. Get away from the Pinnace."

The servant boy was gone in an instant, but not before he'd dropped some hardtack and a piece of junk into my hand.

WEDNESDAY 24th TO THURSDAY 25th *[Plymouth]*
More wind and rain, and the air thick and heavy on my chest. I stink worse than a London gutter. I wish I could just shut my eyes and sleep until everything was right again.

I told Francis Haite about the servant boy who found me.

"That would be John Charlton," Francis Haite said. "He's a good lad. He won't give you up."

Francis Haite is an old man, older than the Captain, with crooked and missing teeth and a face well lined. He clasped my shoulder for a moment. "Be patient, lad," he said.

I shall be patient. Father thinks me worthless when it comes to sticking with a plan. He says I run from everything. Well, I did run from Reverend Smythe's school. And from the Butcher. But I had good cause on both counts. And unhappy as I am, cramped in the hard confines of the Pinnace, I am better off than I was with the Butcher. And so I shall remain, recording my trials in this journal. I shall prove to Father that I am not a quitter. That I am good for something. That I am more than a Butcher's boy.

Finally, the rain has stopped. Empty casks taken off. Fresh supplies of Beer and Water brought on. This afternoon, at last, we weighed anchor. Now there are new sounds to join with the others. The wind clapping the sails, the men singing out in the rigging, the water churned by *Endeavour*'s prow. Fine sounds. Sailing sounds.

FRIDAY 26th *[Off the Coast of England]* Samuel Evans, who has the largest hands I have ever seen, larger even than the Butcher's, found me at my journal, which has suffered from the damp despite its wrappings. He cannot read nor write and thinks it wondrous that a boy of eleven can do what a grown man cannot. "I could teach you," I told him, "when I am out of hiding."

He laughed and nodded his large head. "Time does sit heavy on a seaman some days. It'd be a blessing to read away the hours."

SATURDAY 27th *[Off the Coast, North Atlantic]*

Fair-haired John Ramsay, the youngest of the three men helping me, shipped out the first time when he was but eight.

There are several Gentlemen aboard. I often hear the name of Mr. Banks called. He's a very educated man from the sound of him. His brown hair goes wild in the wind, and his dark eyes are lit with an eager curiosity. Mr. Banks's Company watched porpoises off the side this afternoon. From my hiding place I could hear their remarks and see the pleasure the Gentlemen took in their sightings. I only wish I might have stood at the rail beside them and seen what they saw.

As I write, the sea is ever in my ears and in my bones. *Endeavour* creaks and groans and sighs as she goes. I creak and groan and sigh, as well, but must do it all in silence.

SUNDAY 28th *[Off the Coast, North Atlantic]* Gale in the night. But today the rain gave way to haze and a light breeze, and I dried out a bit. Mr. Banks and his Gentlemen dipped up some seawater and discussed the creatures found swimming in it. The Gentlemen were full of exclamation and wonder.

MONDAY 29th TO TUESDAY 30th *[Off the Coast, North Atlantic]* The weather has turned foul again, and the ship heaves and tosses. I am sick. The Gentlemen have been sick, too. Been at the side regularly. I can say now that Gentlemen heave the contents of their stomach same as eleven-year-old stowaways.

WEDNESDAY 31st TO THURSDAY 1st SEPTEMBER *[Lat. 44° 56' N, Long. 9° 9' W]* All day the sea rose, breaking over the deck. Captain had the men everywhere in the rigging, trying to save the ship from being torn to pieces by the wind.

Just before first watch the Bosun staggered to the side and shook his fist at the sea, cursing it for stealing his skiff. But ship's cook, Mr. Thompson, was angrier still. A dozen of his hens drowned in the storm. Mr. Thompson kept muttering how he was never to feed the entire Company if the sea kept killing his livestock. I'd never seen ship's cook so close before. He has but one hand!

The storm, at last, is blown out and *Endeavour* floats easy in the sea again. The servant boy, John Charlton, comes past when he can, leaving bits to eat. He also brings with him good cheer with that kind face of his and that beaming smile. I don't know much about him but that he is from London, has a friendly nature, and at fifteen years of age has spent his last three years at sea.

He says my red hair reminds him of his mother. He knows his way about, John Charlton does, and he knows the men who brought me aboard. They can be trusted, he said. They're good men.

The men at night sing songs of Spain, and John Charlton says soon we are passing there. He brought me the latitude and longitude readings so I might enter them in my journal and has promised to do so whenever he can. I asked John what I should do about coming out.

"Stay hidden," he said. "If you are discovered now," he said, "Captain may yet put you off on land and see you returned to England."

FRIDAY 2nd *[Between Cape Finisterre and Cape Ortegal]* Spain! I cannot see it from my hiding place, but I heard the cry. The Gentlemen brought their casting nets out and fetched in such creatures I can only imagine. Great were their exclamations of wonder. Their excitement makes my hiding so much more difficult to bear. That and the dampness of it all.

SATURDAY 3rd *[Off the Coast of Spain]* Saw little of the Gentlemen on deck today. At times they are careless and leave a morsel, spiced meat or cheese. Mr. Parkinson, one of the artists Mr. Banks brought aboard to draw the plants and animals we shall see on this voyage, is particularly forgetful with his food. He is a young man with a woman's hands. I am always interested to hear his observations. He speaks in a clear, light voice unlike any other on board. I have seen much in my imagination, listening to Mr. Parkinson's reflections.

SUNDAY 4th *[Off the Coast of Spain]* As the sun was setting, the Gentlemen spied an endless field of little crabs feeding upon the surface of the sea. They cast their net and brought in a dripping lot of the little scuttlers. On deck the crabs glistened in the last rays of sunlight, clicking and slipping over one another. The Gentlemen exclaimed excitedly, and Mr. Banks could not gather the creatures fast enough.

MONDAY 5th *[Off Cape Finisterre]* Mr. Banks received a bird from one of the sailors this morning. It has been tangled in the rigging. The bird died in Mr. Banks's hands. He had one of his servants rush it to Mr. Parkinson to be drawn. I like all animals, but birds are my favourites. The year after Mother died, when I lived with Grandmother, I would climb trees and watch the birds in their nests. I learned to imitate their calls, so that they would come almost to my hand.

Mr. Banks has two greyhound dogs aboard. They

sniff at my hiding place in the shelter of the Pinnace. Ordinarily the sight of them would gladden me, but I fear the bad turn they could do me now if they should give me away. But with the pens of livestock around me, no one questions their excitement. Must be the pigs making them act so, Mr. Banks says.

SILENT TO THE BONE

Ages 10 and Up

Did THIRTEEN-YEAR-OLD BRANWELL cause his half sister's coma? That's what the baby's nanny claims. Is it true? No one knows because Branwell has not uttered a sound since the incident. He can't—or won't—say a word to anyone. Now it's up to his best friend, Connor—the narrator of this thought-provoking and multilayered story—to break through Branwell's silence and find out what really happened on that fateful day.

E. L. KONIGSBURG has written numerous novels, short stories, picture books, and biographies for young readers. She has won the Newbery Medal twice, for *From the Mixed-up Files of Mrs. Basil E. Frankweiler* and *The View from Saturday*. Her first novel, *Jennifer, Hecate, Macbeth, William McKinley, and Me, Elizabeth* was awarded a Newbery Honor.

SILENT TO THE BONE

Excerpt: Chapter 1

E. L. Konigsburg

**I**T IS EASY TO PINPOINT THE MINUTE when my friend Branwell began his silence. It was Wednesday, November 25, 2:43 P.M., Eastern Standard Time. It was there—or, I guess you could say not there—on the tape of the 911 call.

<u>Operator</u>: *Epiphany 911. Hobson speaking.*
SILENCE.
<u>Operator</u>: *Epiphany 911. Hobson. May I help you?*
SILENCE. [Voices are heard in the background.]
<u>Operator</u>: *Anyone there?*
<u>A woman's voice</u> [screaming in the background]: *Tell them. Tell them.*
<u>Operator</u>: *Ma'am, I can't hear you.* [then louder] *Please come to the phone.*
<u>A woman's voice</u> [still in the background, but louder now]: *Tell them.* [then, screaming as the voice approaches] *For God's sake, Branwell.* [the voice gets louder] *TELL THEM.*
SILENCE.

Operator: *Please speak into the phone.*

A woman's voice [heard more clearly]: *TELL THEM.
NOW, BRAN. TELL THEM NOW.*

SILENCE.

A woman's voice with a British accent [heard clearly]:
Here! Take her! For God's sake, at least take her! [then,
speaking directly into the phone] *It's the baby. She
won't wake up.*

Operator: *Stay on the phone.*

British Accent [frightened]: *The baby won't wake up.*

Operator: *Stay on the line. We're transferring you to
Fire and Rescue.*

Male Voice: *Epiphany Fire and Rescue. Davidson. What
is the nature of your emergency?*

British Accent: *The baby won't wake up.*

Male Voice: *What is your exact location?*

British Accent: *198 Tower Hill Road. Help, please. It's
the baby.*

Male Voice: *Help is on the way, ma'am. What
happened?*

British Accent: *He dropped her. She won't wake up.*

Male Voice: *Is she having difficulty breathing?*

British Accent [panicky now]: *Yes. Her breathing is all
strange.*

Male Voice: *How old is the baby, ma'am?*

British Accent: *Almost six months.*

Male Voice: *Is there a history of asthma or heart trouble?*

British Accent: *No, no. He dropped her, I tell you.*

LOUD BANGING IS HEARD.

British Accent [into the phone]: *They're here. Thank God. They're here.* [then just before the connection is broken] *For God's sake, Branwell, MOVE. Open the door.*

The SILENCES were Branwell's. He is my friend.

The baby was Nicole—called Nikki—Branwell's half sister.

The British accent was Vivian Shawcurt, the babysitter.

In the ambulance en route to the hospital, Vivian sat up front with the driver, who was also a paramedic. He asked her what had happened. She told him that she had put the baby down for her afternoon nap and had gone to her room. After talking to a friend on the phone, she had started to read and must have dozed off. When the paramedic asked her what time that was, she had to confess she did not know. The next thing she remembered being awakened by Branwell's screaming for her.

Something was wrong with the baby. When she came into the nursery, she saw Branwell shaking Nikki, trying to get her to wake up. She guessed that the baby went unconscious when he dropped her. She started to do CPR and told Branwell to call 911. He did, but when the operator came on the line, he seemed paralyzed. He would not give her the information she needed. He would not speak at all.

Meanwhile the paramedic who rode with the baby in the ambulance was following the ABC's for resuscitation—airway, breathing, and circulation. Once inside the trauma center at Clarion County Hospital, Nikki was put on a respirator and wrapped in blankets. It was important to keep her warm. A CAT scan was taken of her head, which showed that her injuries could cause her brain to swell. When the brain swells, it pushes against the skull, and that squeezes the blood vessels that supply the brain. If the supply of blood to the brain is pinched off, the brain cannot get oxygen, and it dies.

The doctor drilled a hole in Nikki's skull and put in a small tube—no thicker than a strand of spaghetti—to drain excess fluid from her brain to lower the pressure. Nikki did not open her eyes.

Later that afternoon, a police car arrived at 198

Tower Hill Road and took Branwell to the Clarion
County Juvenile Behavioral Center. He said nothing.
Nothing to the doctors. Nothing to his father, to his step-
mother. Calling to Vivian was the last that Branwell had
spoken. He had not uttered a sound since dialing 911.

Dr. Zamborska, Branwell's father, asked me to visit
him at the Behavioral Center and see if I could get him
to talk. I am Connor, Connor Kane, and—except for the
past six weeks or so—Branwell and I had always been
best friends.

When Dr. Z called me, he reported that the pressure
in Nikki's skull was dropping, and that was a good sign,
but, he cautioned, she was still in a coma. She was in
critical condition, and there was no way of knowing what
the outcome would be.

I was not allowed to see Branwell until Friday, the
day after Thanksgiving. On that first visit to the
Behavioral Center and on all the visits that followed, I
had to stop at a reception desk and sign in. There I
would empty my pockets and, when I had my backpack
with me, I would have to open it as well. If I had nothing that could cause harm to Branwell or could let him
cause harm to someone else (I never did), I was allowed
to put it all back and take it with me.

The first time the guard brought Branwell into the visitors' room, he looked awful. His hair was greasy and uncombed, and he was so pale that the orange jumpsuit he wore cast an apricot glow up from his chin just as his red hair seemed to cast the same eerie glow across his forehead. He shuffled as he walked toward me. I saw that his shoes had no laces. I guessed they had taken them from him.

Branwell is tall for his age—I am not—and when he sat across the table from me, I had to look up to make eye contact, which was not easy. His eyeglasses were so badly smudged that his blue eyes appeared almost gray. It was not at all like him to be uncombed and have his glasses smeared like that. I guessed the smudges were to keep him from seeing out, just as his silence was to keep him from speaking out.

On that first awful, awkward visit, a uniformed guard stood leaning against the wall, watching us. There was no one else in the visitors' room, and I was the only one talking, so everything I said, every sound I made, seemed to echo off the walls. I felt so responsible for getting Branwell to talk that I asked him a bunch of dumb questions. Like: What happened? And: Was there anything he wanted to tell me? He, of course, didn't utter a sound.

Zombielike, he slowly, slowly, slowly shook his head once, twice, three times. This was not the Branwell I knew, and yet, strangely, it was.

Dr. Zamborska had asked me to visit Bran because he figured that I probably knew Branwell better than anyone else in Epiphany—except for himself. And because we had always seemed to have a lot to say to each other. We both loved to talk, but Branwell loved it more. He loved words. He had about five words for things that most people had only one word for, and could use four or five in a single sentence. Dr. Z probably figured that if anyone could get Bran to talk, it would be me. Talk was like the vitamins of our friendship: Large daily doses kept it healthy.

But when Dr. Z had asked me to visit Branwell, he didn't know that about six weeks before that 911 call something had changed between us. I didn't know what caused it, and I didn't exactly know how to describe it. We had not had a fight or even a quarrel, but ever since Monday, Columbus Day, October 12, something that had always been between us no longer was. We still walked to the school bus stop together, we still got off at the same stop, and we still talked. But Branwell never seemed to start a conversation anymore. He not only had less for me, he also had less to say to me, which in terms of our friendship, was pretty much the same thing. He seemed to have something hidden.

We had both turned thirteen within three weeks of each other, and at first I wondered if he was entering a new phase of development three weeks ahead of me. Was something happening to him that would happen to me three weeks later? Had he started to shave? I looked real close. He hadn't. (I was relieved.) Had he become a moody teenager, and would I become one in three more weeks? Three weeks passed, and I didn't. Then six weeks passed—the six weeks between Columbus Day and that 911 call—and I still had not caught the moodiness that was deepening in my friend. And I still did not know what was happening to Bran.

After that first strange, clouded visit, I decided that if I was going back (and I knew that I would), nothing good was going to come out of my visits unless I forgot about our estrangement, forgot about having an assignment from Dr. Z, and acted like the old friend I was.

Once on our way to the school bus stop in the days when Branwell was still starting conversations, he asked me a famous question: "If a tree falls in the forest and no one is there to hear it, does it make a sound?" When he asked me, I couldn't answer and neither could he, but when I left him that first Friday of his long silence, I thought that Branwell could answer it. On that day and for all the days that followed when he made no sound, my friend Branwell was screaming on the inside. And no one heard.

Except me.

So when Branwell at last broke his silence, I was there. I was the first to hear him speak. He spoke to me because even before I know the details, I believed in him. I knew that Branwell did not hurt that baby.

I won't say what his first words were until I explain what I heard during the time he said nothing.